Ricky Ricotta's Mighty Robot Adventures

Three Adventures by
DAV PILKEY
Pictures by
MARTIN ONTIVEROS

SCHOLASTIC INC.

New York Toronto London Auckland Sydney
Mexico City New Delhi Hong Kong Buenos Aires

For Walter Bain Wills — D. P.

To my mom and my family, to all of my friends everywhere
(you know who you are), for their love and support,
and most of all to Micki, and our two kitties,
Bunny and Spanky — M. O.

Ricky Ricotta's Mighty Robot was originally published
in hardcover by the Blue Sky Press in 2000.

ISBN 0-590-30720-7

10 9 8 7 6 5 4 3 2 1   03 04 05 06 07

Printed in the United States of America   40

This compilation first published in March 2003

Ricky Ricotta's Mighty Robot

The First Robot Adventure Novel by
DAV PILKEY
Pictures by
MARTIN ONTIVEROS

Originally published as RICKY RICOTTA'S GIANT ROBOT

SCHOLASTIC INC.
New York Toronto London Auckland Sydney
Mexico City New Delhi Hong Kong Buenos Aires

Chapters

CHAPTER 1

Ricky

There once was a mouse named Ricky Ricotta who lived in Squeakyville with his mother and father.

Ricky liked living with
his mother and father, but
sometimes he got lonely.

Ricky wished he had a friend
to keep him company.

"Don't worry," said Ricky's father.
"Some day something **BIG** will
happen, and you will find a friend."
So Ricky waited.

8

CHAPTER 2

The Bullies

Ricky liked school, but he did not like walking to school. This was because Ricky was very small, and sometimes bullies picked on him.

"Where do you think you are going?" asked one of the bullies.

Ricky did not answer. He
turned and started to run.

DAILY SQUEAK
Strange
Electric
Storms over
Mountains

The bullies chased him.

They knocked Ricky down
and threw his backpack
into a garbage can.

Every day, the bullies chased Ricky.
Every day, they knocked him down.
And every day, Ricky wished that
something **BIG** would happen.

CHAPTER 3

Dr. Stinky McNasty

That day at school, Ricky
ate lunch by himself. Then
he went outside for recess.

He watched the other mice
play a game of kickball.
Ricky did not know that
something **BIG** was about
to happen, but it *was*!

In a secret cave above
the city, a mad doctor was
planning something evil.

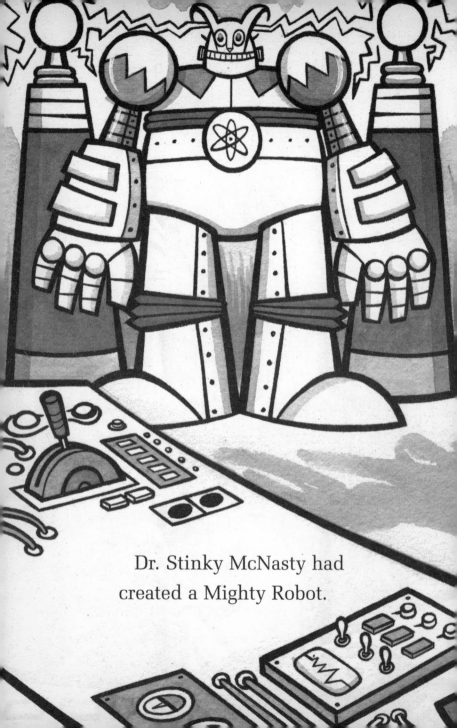

Dr. Stinky McNasty had
created a Mighty Robot.

"I will use this Robot to destroy the city," said Dr. Stinky, "and soon, I will rule the world!"

Dr. Stinky led his Mighty
Robot into town.

"Robot," said Dr. Stinky, "I
want you to **jump** and **stomp**
and *destroy this city*!"

CHAPTER 4

The Mighty Robot

(IN FLIP-O-RAMA™)

O-RAMA

HERE'S HOW IT WORKS!

STEP 1
Place your *left* hand inside the dotted lines marked "LEFT HAND HERE." Hold the book open *flat*.

STEP 2
Grasp the *right-hand* page with your right thumb and index finger (inside the dotted lines marked "RIGHT THUMB HERE").

STEP 3
Now *quickly* flip the right-hand page back and forth until the picture appears to be *animated*.

(For extra fun, try adding your own sound-effects!)

FLIP-O-RAMA 1

(pages 25 and 27)

Remember, flip *only* page 25.
While you are flipping, be sure
you can see the picture on page 25
and the one on page 27.
If you flip quickly, the two
pictures will start to look like
<u>one</u> *animated* picture.

Don't forget to add
your own sound-effects!

LEFT HAND HERE

The Robot Jumped.

25

The Robot Jumped.

FLIP-O-RAMA 2

(pages 29 and 31)

Remember, flip *only* page 29.
While you are flipping, be sure
you can see the picture on page 29
and the one on page 31.
If you flip quickly, the two
pictures will start to look like
<u>one</u> *animated* picture.

Don't forget to add
your own sound-effects!

LEFT HAND HERE

The Robot Stomped.

RIGHT
THUMB
HERE

30

The Robot Stomped.

FLIP-O-RAMA 3

(pages 33 and 35)

Remember, flip *only* page 33.
While you are flipping, be sure
you can see the picture on page 33
and the one on page 35.
If you flip quickly, the two
pictures will start to look like
<u>one</u> *animated* picture.

Don't forget to add
your own sound-effects!

LEFT HAND HERE

But the Robot Would Not Destroy the City.

RIGHT
THUMB
HERE

But the Robot Would Not
Destroy the City.

CHAPTER 5

Ricky to the Rescue

Dr. Stinky was very angry.

"Destroy Squeakyville!" he cried. "Destroy Squeakyville!" But the Robot refused.

"I will teach you a lesson," said Dr. Stinky. He pressed a button on his remote control and zapped the Robot with a terrible shock.

Ricky was watching.

"Stop it!" Ricky cried. But Dr.
Stinky kept on zapping the Robot.
Finally, Ricky aimed a kickball
at the evil doctor. Ricky kicked
as hard as he could.

BOING!

The kickball bounced
off Dr. Stinky's head. Dr.
Stinky dropped the controller,
and it broke on the ground.

"Rats! Rats! *RATS!*" cried Dr. Stinky. "I shall return!" And he disappeared down a sewer drain.

When the Robot saw what Ricky
had done, he walked over to Ricky.
Everyone screamed and ran.

But Ricky was not afraid. The Robot smiled and patted Ricky on the head.

Something **BIG** had happened after all!

CHAPTER 6

Ricky's Pet Robot

That afternoon, the Robot followed Ricky home from school.

Soon they got to Ricky's
house. "Wait here, Robot," said
Ricky. Ricky went inside.

"Mom, Dad," said Ricky, "can I have a pet?"

"Well," said Ricky's father, "you've been a good mouse lately."

"Yes," said Ricky's mother, "I think a pet would be good for you."

"Hooray!" said Ricky.
"Uh-oh," said Ricky's parents.

CHAPTER 7

Ricky's Mighty Robot Helps Out

When Ricky's parents saw Ricky's new pet, they were not happy.

"That Robot is too big to be a pet," said Ricky's father.

"There is no room for him in our home," said Ricky's mom.

"But he is my friend,"
said Ricky, "and he will
help us around the house!"

Ricky's Mighty Robot used
his super breath to blow all
the leaves out of their yard.
Ricky's dad liked that.

Ricky's Robot scared all the crows
out of the vegetable garden.
Ricky's mom liked that.

And when burglars drove
by the Ricottas' house,
they kept right on driving.
Everybody liked that!

"Well," said Ricky's father,
"I guess your Robot can live
in the garage."

"Hooray!" said Ricky.

CHAPTER 8

Back to School

The next day, Ricky and his Robot walked to school. The bullies were waiting for Ricky.

"Where do you think you're going?" asked one of the bullies.

"My Robot and I are going
to school," said Ricky.
The bullies looked up and
saw Ricky's Mighty Robot.
They were very frightened.

"Um . . . um . . . um . . ." said
one of the bullies, "can we carry
your backpack for you, sir?"

"Sure," said Ricky.

The bullies helped Ricky get to
school safely.

"Is there anything else we can
do for you, sir?" asked the bullies.

"No, thank you," said Ricky.

CHAPTER 9
Show-and-Tell

That day at school, Ricky's class had show-and-tell. One mouse brought a baseball glove. Another mouse brought a teddy bear.

Ricky brought his Mighty Robot.

Ricky's class got a free
ride on the Robot's back.

They flew up above the city
and over the mountains.

"This is fun!" said Ricky.

CHAPTER 10

Dr. Stinky's Revenge

While Ricky's class was flying around in the sky, Dr. Stinky sneaked over to the school. He wanted revenge!

Dr. Stinky crept into Ricky's
classroom. He saw their pet lizard.
"This is just what I need!" said
Dr. Stinky.

He took out a bottle of Hate
Potion #9 and put a drop
into the lizard's water dish.
The lizard drank the water.

Suddenly, the lizard began to grow and change. He got bigger and bigger. He got meaner and meaner.

Soon, the lizard turned into
an evil monster.

"Destroy Ricky and his Robot!"
said Dr. Stinky.

"Yes, Master!" said the monster.

When Ricky's Robot saw
the evil monster, he flew down
to the schoolyard. Ricky and
his class climbed off quickly.
Then, the Robot turned toward
the giant monster, and the
battle began.

CHAPTER 11

The Big Battle

(IN FLIP-O-RAMA™)

FLIP-O-RAMA 4

(pages 73 and 75)

Remember, flip *only* page 73.
While you are flipping, be sure
you can see the picture on page 73
and the one on page 75.
If you flip quickly, the two
pictures will start to look like
<u>one</u> *animated* picture.

Don't forget to add
your own sound-effects!

LEFT HAND HERE

The Monster
Attacked.

74

The Monster Attacked.

FLIP-O-RAMA 5

(pages 77 and 79)

Remember, flip *only* page 77.
While you are flipping, be sure
you can see the picture on page 77
and the one on page 79.
If you flip quickly, the two
pictures will start to look like
<u>one</u> *animated* picture.

Don't forget to add
your own sound-effects!

LEFT HAND HERE

Ricky's Robot
Fought Back.

RIGHT
THUMB
HERE

Ricky's Robot
Fought Back.

FLIP-O-RAMA 6

(pages 81 and 83)

Remember, flip *only* page 81.
While you are flipping, be sure
you can see the picture on page 81
and the one on page 83.
If you flip quickly, the two
pictures will start to look like
<u>one</u> *animated* picture.

Don't forget to add
your own sound-effects!

LEFT HAND HERE

The Monster
Battled Hard.

81

82

The Monster
Battled Hard.

FLIP-O-RAMA 7

(pages 85 and 87)

Remember, flip *only* page 85.
While you are flipping, be sure
you can see the picture on page 85
and the one on page 87.
If you flip quickly, the two
pictures will start to look like
<u>one</u> *animated* picture.

Don't forget to add
your own sound-effects!

LEFT HAND HERE

Ricky's Robot
Battled Harder.

85

RIGHT
THUMB
HERE

Ricky's Robot
Battled Harder.

FLIP-O-RAMA 8

(pages 89 and 91)

Remember, flip *only* page 89.
While you are flipping, be sure
you can see the picture on page 89
and the one on page 91.
If you flip quickly, the two
pictures will start to look like
<u>one</u> *animated* picture.

Don't forget to add
your own sound-effects!

LEFT HAND HERE

Ricky's Robot
Saved the Day.

RIGHT
THUMB
HERE

RIGHT
INDEX
FINGER
HERE

Ricky's Robot
Saved the Day.

CHAPTER 12

The Electro-Rocket

The monster was defeated, and all of his evil powers went away. Soon, he turned back into a tiny lizard and never bothered anybody again.

"Rats! Rats! *RATS!*" cried Dr.
Stinky. "I will destroy that Robot
myself!" He took his Electro-Rocket
and aimed it at Ricky's Robot.

"NO!" screamed Ricky. He
leaped onto Dr. Stinky just as
the evil doctor fired his rocket.

Up, up, up went the rocket.
Ricky's Robot flew after it.
But he was not fast enough.

The rocket came down and
exploded.

Ka-BOOM!

Right on Dr. Stinky's secret cave.

CHAPTER 13

Justice Prevails

"Rats! Rats! *RATS!*" cried Dr. Stinky. "This has been a bad day for me!"

"It is about to get worse," said Ricky.

Ricky's Mighty Robot
picked up Dr. Stinky and
put him in the city jail.

CHAPTER 14

Back Home

That night, the Ricotta family had a cookout in the backyard. Ricky told his mom and dad all about their adventures that day.

"Thank you for saving the city," said Ricky's father.

"And thank you for saving each other," said Ricky's mother.

"No problem," said Ricky . . .

. . . "that's what friends are for."

HOW TO DRAW RICKY'S ROBOT

1.

2.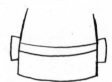

3.

4.

5.

6.

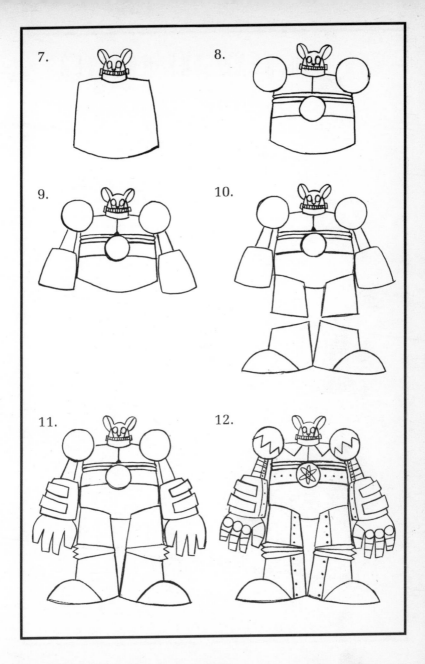

107

HOW TO DRAW THE MONSTER

1.

2.

3.

4.

5.

6.

7.

8.

9.

10.

11.

12.

About the Author and Illustrator

DAV PILKEY created his first stories as comic books while he was in elementary school. In 1997, he wrote and illustrated his first adventure novel for children, *The Adventures of Captain Underpants*, which received rave reviews and was an instant bestseller—as were the three books that followed in the series. Dav is also the creator of numerous award-winning picture books, including *The Paperboy*, a Caldecott Honor Book, and the Dumb Bunnies books. He and his dog live in Portland, Oregon.

It was a stroke of luck when Dav discovered the work of artist **MARTIN ONTIVEROS**. Dav knew that Martin was just the right illustrator for the Ricky Ricotta's Mighty Robot series. Martin also lives in Portland, Oregon. He has a lot of toys as well as two cats, Bunny and Spanky.

Ricky Ricotta's Mighty Robot vs. the Mutant Mosquitoes from Mercury